Published 1983 by
The Hamlyn Publishing Group Limited
London · New York · Sydney · Toronto
Astronaut House, Feltham, Middlesex, England

ISBN 0 600 38853 0

Printed in Italy

The Adventures of
Splodge Pig

Sally Sheringham

Illustrated by Douglas Hall

Hamlyn

London·New York·Sydney·Toronto

Contents

Splodge and Camel

Splodge was a pig. He was white with black splodges, which was why he was called Splodge. He lived at Lemon Tree Farm with lots of other pigs.

Every day, Splodge lay in the sun, closed his eyes and pretended he was in a jungle having adventures with exciting wild animals like gorillas and crocodiles. You see, he didn't like living on the farm with the other pigs very much as he thought they were stupid and boring.

The other pigs didn't like living with Splodge very much, either. 'You're a fat, lazy, useless animal, Splodge Pig,' they said. 'Haven't you got anything better to do than lie in the sun all day?'

'No, I haven't, actually,' said Splodge, not bothering to open his eyes.

'Rude as well as fat and lazy and useless,' snorted the pigs. 'Really, your poor mother must despair of you.'

And his mother *did* despair of him. 'Why can't you behave decently like any other pig, Splodge?' she said.

'Because I'm not like any other pig, Mum, you know that,' said Splodge. 'I am a pig with a brain, but I never get the chance to use it. Even though you and the other pigs are happy to spend your lives on a boring farm, I'm not. I want to have exciting adventures, meet clever wild animals like gorillas and crocodiles against whom I can pit my wits.'

'What nonsense, Splodge,' said Splodge's mother. 'Why, a gorilla or crocodile would gobble you up quicker than you could say "acorns".'

'Even that would be better than
dying of boredom,' said Splodge
gloomily.

His mother said that that was the
silliest thing he'd said yet. 'You have
a good home here, with a kind
farmer who gives you plenty to eat,'
she said. 'Just be grateful for what
you've got.'

But Splodge wasn't.

One day, a colourful bird called a bee-eater landed on the fence for a rest. Splodge opened one eye. 'Hello,' he said. 'Can you tell me, please, how far it is to the nearest jungle full of wild animals?'

'Certainly,' said the bee-eater. 'It is a long, long way away, on the other side of the Great Hot White Desert. Unless you are a bird or a camel, you will never get across alive. Anyway, even if you were to,' continued the bird, 'you would be eaten by the cruel tigers who have arrived and now rule the jungle. All the animals, even the crocodiles, are frightened of them.'

Splodge opened his other eye. 'Thank you, Bee-eater. That is most interesting,' he said. 'Even if I never get across the Great Hot White Desert, at least I can now lie here dreaming about ridding the jungle of the tigers.'

The bee-eater laughed and flew away.

But time went on, and Splodge grew tired of dreaming. Dreams were all very well but they weren't the same as actually *doing* things. But how on earth was he ever going to cross the Great Hot White Desert?

One day he was looking across the farmyard when he suddenly saw something amazing. He blinked once and then twice. Was this one of his dreams, or could he really see a camel walking towards him? 'Trembling trotters!' said Splodge. 'It really is a camel!'

'How do you do,' he said, very excited. 'I'm Splodge Pig and I've always wanted to meet a real wild animal like you.'

'Oh,' said Camel. 'I'm not really a *wild* animal. Or perhaps I am now, it all depends. I'm in a bit of a jam, you see. I've escaped from my cruel master but he's out looking for me, and I badly need a place to hide till nightfall.'

Splodge looked round. There weren't any good hiding places on the farm. Then he had an idea. 'If you lie down and tuck your head in, I can lean on you and pretend to be asleep. Only your hump will show, and it'll look just like a rock.'

'What a splendid idea,' said Camel.

So that's what they did, and everyone was so used to seeing Splodge sleeping against rocks that they didn't look twice. Neither did the cruel master who came looking for Camel.

At nightfall, when all the other pigs were asleep and the farmer's curtains were drawn, Splodge whispered, 'The coast is clear.' Then he moved so that Camel could unbend and stand up.

'Phew, what a relief,' said Camel. 'I was getting a bit tired of being a rock. And now Splodge, if there's anything I can do to repay you for your kindness, I would be happy to do it.'

'Well, there is one thing,' said Splodge. 'You aren't going anywhere near the Great Hot White Desert, are you? You see, I would very much like to visit the jungle ruled by tigers.'

'As a matter of fact,' said Camel, 'I am. I'll be glad of the company. You can sit on my hump.'

'I won't be too heavy, will I?' asked Splodge. 'You've probably noticed that I am rather plump.'

Camel laughed. 'You'll be as light as a feather compared to some of the things my master loaded on to my back,' he said. 'Once I had to carry more than a hundred bricks. But we mustn't waste any more time.'

So Splodge quickly packed his possessions in his little red satchel: a white cotton sunhat, a green unblown-up balloon that he'd picked up in the farmyard, a firework and some bangers that he'd found after a fireworks party. He also packed an emergency supply of acorns and a bottle of water in a suitcase.

Then he wrote in large letters on the wall of the pigsty: HAVE GONE TO GET RID OF THE TIGERS. DON'T WORRY ABOUT ME. LOVE SPLODGE PIG.

'Right, on you get,' said Camel, bending his knees.

Splodge sat on Camel's hump. But how odd it felt as Camel started to walk – like being on top of a tiny rocking mountain! He found it very difficult to stay on.

As they walked out of the farmyard, Splodge felt a tiny bit sad. After all, Lemon Tree Farm had been his home all his life. And then he remembered – his adventures were about to start. This wasn't a dream. It was really happening!

Camel kept well away from the towns and the villages. 'After all, a pig with a red satchel riding on the back of a camel will attract attention,' he said sensibly.

All night they travelled, and then all day. It got hotter and hotter, and Splodge's white patches turned rather pink. Soon, there were no more fields, just barren, rocky ground. Then, suddenly, ahead of them they could see the Great Hot White Desert stretching on and on for ever.

'Hurray!' shouted Splodge. 'The adventure's really beginning now.'

'Hurray!' shouted Camel. 'My master will never come looking for me here, and soon I'll be reunited with my family. Now I must have a drink.' He found a large water-hole, and drank – and drank – and drank. Splodge thought he'd drink every single drop! 'Won't you burst?' he asked anxiously.

Camel laughed. 'No, I've still got some room left,' he said. 'But that should be enough to get me across the desert.' Then, as he began to walk across the white sand Camel said, 'If you don't mind me asking, why do you want to go to the jungle? It's a very dangerous place for a pig, you know.'

Splodge explained that that was why he wanted to go. 'I want a few challenges, you see,' he said. 'Life on Lemon Tree Farm was so very dull.'

32

'Well, you must be very careful, Splodge. There are some dangerous, some very dangerous and some *extremely* dangerous animals living in the jungle,' said Camel. 'For example, I think I'm right in saying that gorillas and monkeys are dangerous, snakes and crocodiles are very dangerous and the tigers are *extremely* dangerous.'

'Thank you, I'll bear that in mind,' said Splodge.

On and on they journeyed across
the Great Hot White Desert.
Splodge had never seen so much
sand in his life. Nor had he ever
been so hot. He was glad of his
sunhat. One day there was a terrible
sandstorm, so they had to stop and
lie down and close their eyes till it
was over. It was most unpleasant.
Splodge thought it felt as if millions
of tiny acorns were being fired at him
at once.

After several days and several nights, they suddenly saw, in the distance, some camels, and, beyond the camels, the jungle!

'Hold on tight, Splodge,' said Camel, who was terribly excited. 'I'm going to gallop.' And he did. Splodge had to hold on for dear life.

The camels never thought they would see their long-lost brother again, and they wept for joy. Then Camel introduced Splodge to his brothers and sisters and aunts and uncles. They had never met a pig before and made him feel very welcome.

Splodge stayed with the camels for two days. Then he decided it was time to leave. 'Now I must go into the jungle,' he said, 'for that was the reason for my long journey.'

'Good luck, my dear friend,' said Camel.

39

'When I'm King of the jungle you must come and live with me,' joked Splodge, as he picked up his satchel. Camel laughed, but as he watched Splodge go, getting smaller and smaller till he was just a dot in the distance, a tear rolled down his cheek. 'What a brave little pig,' he said. 'He won't last five minutes among all those hungry wild animals. We'll never see him alive again.' The other camels sadly agreed.

Splodge and the camels could not see the pair of yellow tiger eyes that were glinting hungrily out of the jungle. . .

Splodge learns about the tigers

As Splodge got nearer to the jungle, he felt more and more excited – and more and more nervous, too. Judging by all the different noises coming out of the jungle, it was *bristling with* wild animals.

He began to feel hungry, so he sat under a tree at the edge of the jungle to eat some acorns. Just as he was about to tuck in, an enormous hairy hand grabbed him from behind.

'EEEK!' cried Splodge and looked round to see whose enormous hairy hand it was. He came face to face with a *really* enormous hairy gorilla!

44

'Er – how do you do,' said Splodge nervously. He couldn't remember whether Camel had said that gorillas were dangerous, very dangerous or extremely dangerous. But the gorilla picked him up, threw him over his hairy shoulder as if he were a sack of potatoes, and carried him deep into the heart of the jungle.

45

Splodge had never seen so many pairs of eyes, staring at him from holes in trees and behind branches and out of the undergrowth. 'Trembling trotters! Whatever's going to happen to me?' he wondered.

After what seemed a very long time, they arrived at a clearing. In the middle of the clearing was a water-hole around which a whole collection of animals was gathered. There was a snake, a wild boar, an elephant, an antelope, several monkeys and a parrot. Splodge's eyes bulged at the sight of all these wild animals. None of them *looked* very dangerous.

The gorilla put Splodge down and said, 'I have reason to believe that this er – pig is a spy. I found him at the edge of the jungle trying to listen to my conversation.'

'The pig's a spy! The pig's a spy!' repeated the parrot.

'I'm not a spy,' protested Splodge angrily. 'I'm Mr Splodge Pig of Lemon Tree Farm. I crossed the Great Hot White Desert on the back of a camel in order to get to this jungle. I came to have some adventures and help you all get rid of the tigers.'

The animals laughed. 'And how do you think that you, a small plump pig, will do that?' asked Elephant.

'I don't know yet, but I'm sure I'll think of a way,' said Splodge. 'I have quite a good brain, you know.'

'I'm sure you have,' said Gorilla, scratching his head. 'But we still can't be sure that you haven't been sent by the tigers to spy on us,'

Splodge thought for a moment. Then, opening his satchel, he got out his white cotton sunhat. He put it on his head and did a tap dance round the water-hole on the tips of his trotters.

When he had finished he gave a little bow and said, 'Have you ever seen a spy wearing a sunhat and doing a tap dance?'

The animals had to agree that they hadn't.

'I owe you an apology, Splodge,' said Gorilla. 'But you see we have to be suspicious of all strangers. You never know who the tigers are going to have working for them next.'

54

'Don't mention it,' said Splodge, sitting down as he was feeling a bit puffed. 'And now, would you tell me some more about these tigers?'

'They are cruel and evil,' said Antelope.

'Under the command of the wicked King Snarlalot, they rule the jungle,' said Gorilla.

'They make our lives a complete misery,' said Wild Boar.

'They kidnap our babies,' said the monkeys.

'Kidnap our babies! Kidnap our babies!' screamed the parrot.

'How did they arrive here in the first place?' asked Splodge. 'I didn't think tigers normally lived in Africa.'

'They don't, but these aren't normal tigers,' said Gorilla. 'It's a long story and Elephant will tell you if he doesn't mind. He has the best memory of any of us.'

56

'Well,' said Elephant, 'the story goes that the tigers once lived far away in a jungle in India, where they terrified all the other animals who lived there, eating them whenever they felt like it. And then men started to hunt the tigers with guns, so they decided to become pirates.

57

They managed to steal a ship, and off they sailed. Every ship they met they would leap aboard, eat the sailors and then steal all there was to steal – gold and jewels and food and wine. It wasn't long before every sailor on every sea couldn't even think about the tigers without shaking like jellies. They were more afraid of them than of drowning in a storm or of being eaten alive by a shark.

'After a while, the tigers had so many stolen jewels and so much stolen gold on board their ship, that it began to sink. And, just our luck, this happened close to our jungle. So the tigers swam to the shore, bringing the gold and the jewels with them.

'I can remember that dreadful day as if it were yesterday. We all stood watching them coming towards the jungle and every one of us was trembling. Because, you see, we had heard about all the terrible things they'd done at sea and we knew that they'd do the same terrible things to *us* if they came to live in our jungle. We tried to put up a fight, and oh deary me, what a lot of blood was shed that afternoon. We all did our best. Crocodiles snapped, snakes throttled, parrots pecked, hippos charged, antelopes kicked, Gorilla thumped, monkeys threw coconuts, I trampled, and all the other animals did what they could, but with little success. The tigers were just too strong and powerful and fierce for us. It was a dreadful sight to see so many brave animals killed by the tigers. It was a very sad day indeed,' and a tear rolled down Elephant's wrinkled grey cheek.

63

Then he continued: 'When the fighting stopped at last, with much roaring and snarling the tigers announced that from now on they would be the rulers of the jungle.

They then built their castle, a dark, evil place in the darkest, most evil part of the jungle, and painted it in black and yellow stripes. I've never been inside it myself, thankgoodness, but I've heard that the walls are decorated with the heads of the animals they have killed.'

At this, all the animals, including Splodge, shivered.

'They made Snarlalot, the most ferocious of all the tigers, their king,' continued Elephant. 'None of us have had the misfortune to meet him, as he rarely leaves the castle. We've been told, though, that when he's angry, his eyes turn a bright fiery red, and that his teeth are so sharp, he can bite off an elephant's trunk in one go.' Elephant's own trunk trembled before he continued.

'Vultures circle the castle, watching
out for enemies. In return, they are
allowed to pick at the bones of the
animals that the tigers have eaten.
They are truly terrible birds.'

67

'But the most terrible thing of all,' said a monkey, 'is that just lately, the tigers have been stealing our babies. They carry them back to the castle, where they are fattening them up. Any day now they will eat them, and we'll never see our babies again,' and he burst into tears.

'Oh yes you will,' said Splodge. 'Because I am going to think of a way to rescue them. And then I'll see what I can do to get rid of the tigers.'

The animals laughed, though not unkindly. What on earth could a plump pig in a sunhat do to get rid of the tigers? Why, they'd gobble him up for breakfast. Come to think of it, there were several other animals living in the jungle who would gobble him up for breakfast, too.

'Well, you be careful, Splodge,' said Gorilla. 'You'd better stay the night in my house. You see, the jungle is full of danger.'

'Don't worry, I *thrive* on danger,' said Splodge cheerfully, but all the animals shook their heads in wonder at this brave but foolish pig.

The only animal who didn't shake his head in wonder was a tiger, who was well hidden behind some trees. He was too busy licking his lips at the sight of this plump pig. His yellow eyes glinted evilly in the darkness.

Splodge at the river

When Splodge awoke the next morning, he thought at first that he was at Lemon Tree Farm, and that the sharp thing that was digging into his ribs was his mother's trotter. And then he remembered. He was in the jungle full of wild animals, and the sharp thing digging into his ribs was Gorilla's elbow!

'Before I even think about getting rid of the tigers I must first make friends with all the other animals,' he said to himself. So he set off excitedly to look for wild animals.

He hadn't gone very far before he came to a deep, dark river. On the surface of the river he noticed two eyes and two nostrils. The eyes were staring at him.

'I wonder what animal they could belong to,' thought Splodge. 'I'll say good morning to it anyway and hope that it's friendly.'

'Good morning,' he shouted to the staring eyes. 'I'm Mr Splodge Pig and I've travelled across the Great Hot White Desert on the back of a camel in order to rid this jungle of tigers.'

Suddenly, Splodge took a step backwards in fright, for he could now see that the eyes and the nostrils belonged to an exceedingly large crocodile. Her head had come out of the water revealing a mouth full of teeth. Splodge wouldn't have been able to count them all even if he'd had the time.

He smiled nervously, but Crocodile didn't smile back. She never smiled these days. Ever since her baby had been stolen by the tigers she hadn't smiled once. She was now a very sad, bad-tempered crocodile.

'Don't be ridiculous,' snapped the crocodile. 'How can a plump pig rid the jungle of tigers? I've never heard such nonsense. Besides, you won't have the chance because I'm going to gobble you up for my breakfast.'

Splodge's knees wobbled so much
he was in danger of falling into the
river. Other animals watched with
interest from behind bushes or high
up in trees or in the river itself. How-
ever, they wondered, was this pig
going to escape the jaws of the
crocodile?

Splodge looked anxiously at the
open mouth of the crocodile. Why,
three pigs would fit into it with no
trouble. And he didn't like the look
of all those sharp teeth one bit. He
must act fast.

'Er, before you eat me, Crocodile,
I'd like to tell you a crocodile joke, if
I may.'

The crocodile sighed. 'Very well, if you must,' she said. 'But I won't laugh, you know. Actually, I think I've forgotten how to. And please be quick. I'm getting hungry.'

Splodge cleared his throat and squeaked nervously, 'A man goes into a sandwich shop and says : 'Can I have a crocodile sandwich, please, and make it snappy.'

82

For a second, a terrible silence hung over the river. Then the crocodile opened her mouth wide . . . and burst out laughing! All the other animals joined in. What a din! 'Oh, little pig,' Crocodile said, tears streaming down her cheeks, 'I haven't heard anything so funny for years. And I really thought I'd forgotten how to laugh.'

83

'Er – are you still going to eat me for breakfast?' asked Splodge timidly.

'How could I possibly eat someone who makes me laugh,' said Crocodile. 'Thank you, little pig, for making a sad, bad-tempered crocodile a little bit happier,' and she turned and swam away.

Splodge mopped his brow. Phew, that was a narrow escape! Suddenly he caught sight of two more eyes and nostrils, and two ears as well, on the surface of the river. The eyes were staring at him, and they belonged to an animal that had an even larger mouth than the crocodile! Why, it was big enough to fit *five* pigs inside with no trouble.

'Oh dear, you don't want to gobble me up for breakfast too, do you?' asked Splodge.

The hippopotamus – for that was who it was – threw her massive grey head back and laughed. 'No, of course I'm not going to gobble you up, Splodge Pig,' she said. 'I'd just like to congratulate you. I've been trying to make Crocodile laugh for weeks and have failed dismally. You are not only a brave pig but a funny one, too.'

'Hear! Hear!' cried the other animals.

'Hear! Hear! Hear! Hear!' screamed the parrot.

The only animal who didn't say 'hear hear', was a tiger who was growling angrily to himself, his yellow eyes glinting through the trees.

Splodge walked off through the jungle, whistling a cheerful tune. He hadn't gone far, when suddenly he found himself surrounded by angry monkeys.

'Hello,' said Splodge. He smiled nervously, for there were a great many of them, and their teeth looked uncommonly sharp.

'Hello? Don't you mean good-bye?' said the largest and fiercest-looking monkey. 'Who do you think you are, coming into *our* jungle and announcing that you'll get rid of the tigers? That's what we'd like to know. You make it sound as easy as picking bananas off trees. But everyone knows that we monkeys are the cleverest animals in the jungle and that pigs are stupid. If anyone around here is going to get rid of the tigers, it's going to be us.'

'In other words,' said another monkey with a wicked-looking snarl, 'we want you to get out of here.' And he jerked his thumb in the direction of the edge of the jungle.

'Get out of here! Get out of here!' screamed the parrot.

'But wait a minute . . .' said Splodge.

'No buts,' said the monkey with the roughest, gruffest voice. 'We don't want your type round here.'

'Yeah, why don't you go back to the farmyard where you belong?' snarled all the monkeys together.

'Yeah! Yeah!' screamed the parrot.

Splodge was very tempted to burst into tears, but he knew that that was the last thing he should do. So, instead, he took a deep breath and said, 'Before you throw me out of the jungle, why don't we have a competition to see who really is the cleverest?'

The monkeys loved competitions. 'You're on,' said the largest and fiercest monkey. 'But I warn you, you don't stand a chance against us lot. What's the competition?'

Splodge thought quickly. 'The one who can walk across the river without sinking is the cleverest.'

The monkeys looked at him open-mouthed. Surely it wasn't possible.

'Oh well, anything a pig can do we can do better,' said the largest monkey.

'Shall we meet at the bend in the river in, say, an hour's time?' said Splodge. 'And now, if you'll excuse me, I have some business to attend to.'

An hour later, they were all assembled.

'That silly fat pig will sink like a stone,' muttered the monkeys.

'Sink like a stone! Sink like a stone!' screamed the parrot.

'Okay,' shouted Gorilla, who was judge. 'The monkeys are to go first.'

What a splish and a splosh and a splash there was, as first one monkey, then another, tried to walk across the river without sinking. But each of them sank immediately. Soon, a row of wet, bedraggled monkeys stood on the bank. 'Oh well, if we can't do it, neither will that pig,' they told each other.

'And now it's Mr Splodge Pig's turn to attempt to walk across the river,' announced Gorilla.

Splodge walked casually to the water's edge. He dipped one trotter in to test the temperature. Then he stepped off the bank and began to walk across the river *without sinking!* The monkeys' mouths dropped open in amazement. How on earth did he do it?

When Splodge reached the other side, he stood on the bank and gave a small bow. All the animals cheered, and even the monkeys rather reluctantly joined in. Why, this pig wasn't only brave and funny, but clever too.

Only two animals didn't cheer. One was Hippo, because she was hiding in the dark, murky river. If she cheered, not only would her large mouth fill up with water, but she'd give the game away, too. She smiled to herself. She was glad she'd been able to help out the little pig by allowing him to ride on her back.

The other animal who didn't cheer was a tiger. His yellow eyes glinted fiercely.

Splodge has two narrow escapes

Splodge lay in the shade under a tree, smiling to himself. Things were going better than he could have dreamed. How happy he felt. Suddenly, he heard a rustle. He opened his eyes and nearly jumped out of his skin. He was looking straight into the eyes of an enormous, *really* enormous, snake!

'Er, how do you do,' said Splodge. 'I'm Mr Splodge Pig of Lemon Tree Farm and I crossed the Great Hot White Desert in order to rid the jungle of tigers.'

'Did you indeed?' hissed the snake in a snooty voice, and he slid a little closer so that he could have a better view of this plump, tasty-looking pig. 'Well, I'm afraid that even if you were capable of getting rid of the tigers, which you clearly aren't, you won't get the chanssce to do sso.'

'And why is that, Sir?' asked Splodge, his trotters trembling.

'Becaussse I'm about to crush every bone in your body and then eat you for my lunch,' said the snake, as he edged a little closer.

Splodge thought quickly. 'Er, before you do that,' he said, 'can I make a bargain with you? That if I can prove I am stronger than you are, you won't eat me for your lunch?'

The snake threw his head back
and laughed in such a way that
Splodge could see right down his
wide throat. He certainly didn't
want to end up there, thank you very
much.

When the snake had finished laughing, he said, 'Thisss will be mossst amusssing. *Mossst* amusssing. And how, may I asssk, are you going to prove that you are ssstronger than I am?'

'I bet you can't squeeze a water melon so tight that it explodes with a bang,' Splodge said.

The snake laughed again. 'Well, if I can't, you certainly can't either, and that's for sssure. Just look at you. You haven't got a mussscle in your body, and even if you have, it'sss covered in fat.'

'Covered in fat! Covered in fat!' screamed the parrot.

'We shall see about that,' said Splodge. 'I'll meet you back here in half an hour with my water melon.' Then he hurried off to fetch his red satchel. He got out the green balloon, and blew it up till it was the size of a water melon. Then he tied a knot in the end. Smiling to himself, he trotted back to where Snake was waiting with his water melon.

Word had got around about the contest, and a whole crowd of animals had gathered to watch. 'Splodge Pig is never going to win this one,' they all whispered.

'Right,' said Gorilla who was judge once again. 'Snake to go first.'

So Snake wrapped his long, thick body round his water melon and squeezed and strained and squeezed and strained. But, although he tried hard, he didn't get his water melon to explode with a bang. He didn't get it to go 'pop' or even 'splat'. All he did get it to go was a quiet little 'phut'.

'And now it's Mr Splodge Pig's turn,' announced Gorilla.

So Splodge held his 'water melon' between his two front trotters, and pretended to squeeze and strain and squeeze and strain. The animals all shook their heads, and Snake smiled. 'Sssilly weakling of a pig,' he said to himself. 'Fansscy him thinking he'ss sstronger than me.' Suddenly, his smile vanished. For Splodge's water melon had exploded with a really loud BANG!

'BANG! BANG!' screamed the parrot.

Snake was so amazed that the only thing he could think of to say was, 'Well, I never!'

How all the animals cheered. Why, this pig wasn't only brave, funny and clever, he was *strong*, too.

Splodge was just about to take a small bow, when he heard someone shout, 'HELP! HELP'. He ran in the direction the sound was coming from. Suddenly, he saw in front of him a pride of big, fierce lions standing in a circle round a little warthog. It looked as though they were about to eat her.

'Excuse me,' said Splodge bravely. 'My name is Mr Splodge Pig of . . .'

But before he could get any further
the lions dragged him into the middle
of the circle, too.

  'You were saying?' said the leader
of the lions, a cruel smile on his lips.

  'Er – I've come to rid the jungle of
the tigers, you see.'

The lions roared with laughter. Their teeth looked very sharp. 'Well you won't do it, because we are going to eat you and this warthog for our supper,' said the leader of the lions. He was standing so close that Splodge could feel his hot fiery breath on his cheek.

Splodge was so frightened that his tail went straight. 'Oh, please don't. I'm a clever pig and I promise to get rid of the tigers if you don't eat me.'

'So you think you're smarter than us lions, eh? And what do you suppose you can do that we can't, except look fat and stupid?'

Splodge thought fast. Luckily, he still had his satchel with him. 'I can send red, blue and green stars up into the sky,' he said.

At this the lions grew very angry. 'You are a liar, little pig,' they said. 'And we lions don't like liars.'

'Liar! Liar!' screamed the parrot. Splodge said he wasn't a liar, and begged the lions to let him prove that he could send coloured stars up into the sky.

The lions had a quick conference. 'Very well,' said the leader eventually. 'But if it turns out you've been lying to us, you'll experience a truly horrible death. We will start by biting off your tail and then your ears. On the other hand, if you manage to send coloured stars into the sky – which of course you can't – we won't eat you.'

'Or Warthog?' said Splodge.

The lion sighed. 'Oh, all right, or Warthog.'

Splodge explained that they'd have to wait till it got dark or the stars wouldn't show up in the sky. The lions agreed, but they stayed in their circle to make sure their prisoners didn't escape.

So Splodge and Warthog, standing in the middle of a circle of lions, started talking to each other. First, Warthog thanked Splodge for so bravely trying to rescue her.

'Think nothing of it,' said Splodge cheerfully. 'And now tell me about yourself.'

So Warthog told him how the other warthogs were so dull and stupid that she decided to set off on her own in search of adventures, which was when she'd been chased by the lions into the jungle and caught. 'You see, just because I'm a warthog everyone thinks I must be stupid,' she said sadly. 'But I'm not stupid. I just never have the chance to use my brain.'

'I know the feeling exactly,' said Splodge. 'The same thing happened to me. And I promise that if we manage to escape from the lions and rid the jungle of the tigers, I will do all I can to give you the chance to use your brain.'

'Oh, thank you, Splodge,' said Warthog, her knobbled face lighting up. Then it fell again. 'And then there's my other problem. Everyone says I'm so *ugly*.'

'I don't think you're ugly at all. In fact, I would go so far as to say you're very beautiful,' said Splodge, turning a little pink.

At nightfall, an air of excitement spread through the jungle. Splodge Pig had told some lions he could send coloured stars up into the sky! Surely he had gone too far this time. Meanwhile, the lions licked their lips. They were looking forward to plump pig and warthog for supper.

When all the animals in the jungle were gathered, Splodge placed the firework in his water bottle. Then he rubbed two pieces of wood together to create a spark that lit the firework. Whoosh! Up it went, filling the sky with red, blue and green stars.

All the animals gasped, and the lions gasped loudest of all. They had never seen anything like it in their lives. Was this pig a magician, too? While everyone cheered, Warthog nuzzled Splodge's shoulder with her nose. 'You have saved my life,' she said. 'How can I ever thank you enough?'

'Don't mention it,' said Splodge. 'It was a pleasure.'

'Listen everyone,' shouted Gorilla.

'I have an important announcement to make. Splodge Pig walked into the jungle boasting that he could get rid of the tigers. Because he was a pig we all laughed at him. But he has proved that he is not only brave, but funny, clever, strong and even magical as well. I therefore suggest that we listen to his plans on how to get rid of the tigers, and give him our full support in whatever he decides to do. All those in favour say "Ay".'

'Ay,' yelled the monkeys and Hippo, Crocodile and Snake, the wild boars and the frogs, the birds, the antelopes, the elephant and even the lions.

'Ay! Ay!' screamed the parrot.

In fact the only animal who didn't say 'Ay' was a tiger, whose yellow eyes glinted fiercely out of the darkness. And the animals made such a noise cheering Splodge that they didn't hear him snarl angrily before galloping off into the night. . .

Splodge meets King Snarlalot

While Splodge held his meeting to discuss ways to get rid of the tigers, far away in Tiger Castle, the tigers were discussing ways to get rid of Splodge!

136

'He's done nothing but cause
trouble since he arrived in the
jungle,' growled one tiger.

'He wants to get rid of us,' snarled
another.

At this, the tigers laughed. 'What
a nerve he's got, thinking that he, a
mere pig, can get rid of us mighty
tigers.'

'Mind you,' snarled another, 'he is brave.'

'And funny.'

'And clever.'

'And strong.'

'And a magician.'

'And plump.'

The tiger who had said '"and plump' was now smiling in a very cruel way so that all his teeth showed. 'I reckon he would go down extremely well for breakfast, along with some of those baby animals. They must be nice and plump by now. What do you say?'

'Yeah,' shouted all the tigers, licking their lips.

'Come on then,' said the tiger who'd said 'and plump'. 'Let's go and get him.'

At the other meeting, Splodge and the animals were discussing an extremely good plan, when ten terrible tigers burst in. They tossed Splodge into the air like a pancake, and carried him off. There was nothing the animals could do.

140

'Even though he is a remarkable
pig, we'll never see him again,' said
Gorilla sadly. 'No one ever comes
out of Tiger Castle alive.' And all the
animals wept.

Meanwhile, the tigers carried Splodge deeper and deeper into the jungle. They began to throw him from one to another as if he were a ball.

'Please put me down,' cried Splodge. 'You're making me feel sick.'

The tigers just laughed and continued with their game.

Eventually they arrived at Tiger Castle, a huge, frightening place that was painted in black and yellow stripes. The vultures circled overhead. The tigers carried Splodge down dark slimy steps and threw him into the dungeon. Thwack! He landed on something hard that started to cry. 'Sorry,' said Splodge and, when his eyes got used to the dark, he saw that he had landed on Baby Crocodile. All the other baby animals were there, too.

'Hello, I am Splodge Pig,' he said. 'Don't worry, I'll think of a way to get us all out of here.'

'Oh, I do hope so,' squeaked Baby Antelope, 'because we're getting so plump that soon the tigers will eat us.'

145

'Rely on me,' said Splodge and everyone cheered – apart from the guard on duty. His yellow eyes were glinting through the spy hole in the door.

So Splodge began to think of ways to save the baby animals. But the more he thought the more his mind went blank. In fact he couldn't think of anything at all. 'Trembling trotters,' he thought, a tear running down his plump cheek, 'I'm really in a jam this time.' And he was.

Suddenly there was a great rattling of chains and bolts. The door opened and the guard growled, 'King Snarlalot wants to see you, Splodge Pig.'

Splodge was led down corridors whose walls were covered with the heads of the animals the tigers had already eaten. Splodge trembled so much his knees knocked. And, when he came face to face with King Snarlalot, the biggest and most terrible of all the tigers, he thought his teeth would drop out they were chattering so much.

148

The king's eyes turned a bright fiery red he was so angry, and he snarled to reveal the teeth that could bite off an elephant's trunk in one go. Then, giving a loud, ferocious roar that made Splodge's ears ring, he ordered all the guards to leave the room.

When King Snarlalot and Splodge were alone, King Snarlalot roared and growled and snarled a bit more and then, to Splodge's amazement, burst into tears!

'Splodge Pig, I'm a complete fraud,' he said, wiping his eyes on a black and yellow striped handkerchief. 'You see, I'm not really fierce and terrible at all. In fact I'm a coward. I have to *pretend* to be fierce because of the other tigers. They would kill me if they knew the truth.

I don't want to be King Snarlalot at all but would like to lead a quiet, peaceful life growing flowers. I hate the way we rule the jungle but what can I do? I'm in their power, just like you all are.'

'I see,' said Splodge.

'I have heard a lot about you Splodge, and you sound quite a remarkable pig,' continued King Snarlalot. 'If there's anything I can do to help you rid the jungle of these cruel tigers, please let me know.'

Splodge was so astonished he couldn't speak for a while. Then he said, 'Are the tigers frightened of anything?'

King Snarlalot sadly shook his head. 'They are quite fearless,' he said. And then his face brightened. 'Oh, there is one thing. They are terrified that hunters will come into the jungle to shoot them.'

Splodge thought for a moment. Then he said, 'I'm beginning to get an extremely good idea. . .'

Splodge's dream comes true

The tigers were all fast asleep. They were so busy dreaming about eating plump pig for breakfast, that they didn't hear King Snarlalot escort Splodge out of the castle.

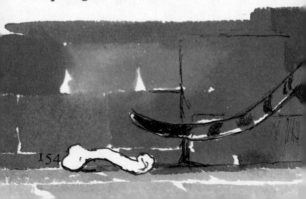

'Good luck, Splodge,' whispered the king when they reached the castle gates. 'I'll keep my claws crossed.'

'Thanks,' said Splodge, and he trotted off into the darkest, most evil part of the jungle.

'Well, so far so good,' Splodge thought to himself. But there was one thing he had forgotten about. Do you know what it was? Yes, the *vultures*. They were perched on the turrets of the castle, having their evening chat.

'I wonder what pig tastes like,' one vulture was saying.

'I don't know, but I can't wait to find out,' said another.

'I guess it tastes like a cross between warthog and antelope,' said a third.

'No,' said a fourth. 'I bet it tastes more like . . .' And then he stopped. 'Well, talk of the devil,' he said. 'Are my eyes deceiving me or can I see that plump pig escaping into the jungle?'

They all peered down and, even though their eyesight wasn't at its best at night, they agreed that they could see Splodge's hindquarters disappearing behind some trees.

159

'Well, lads, what do you say?'
said the fourth vulture. 'Shall we go
and stop him?'

'You bet,' said the second vulture.
'I was really looking forward to
plump pig for breakfast.'

'Same here,' they all said and so,
with a great flap, flap, flap of wings,
they rose from the turrets, swooped
down and surrounded a very startled
Splodge Pig.

'Oh!' he said. That was all he
could think of to say.

'So,' said the vultures, 'you thought you could escape the tigers, did you? Well, you were wrong, because we're going to pick you up and carry you straight back inside the castle again,' and they all cackled loudly. It was such a horrible, frightening sound, that Splodge's snout trembled. He didn't like the thought of being carried back to the castle one bit, and their beaks looked very sharp. He had to think fast.

'Er, actually, I'm not trying to escape the tigers,' he said. 'You see I've agreed to become their spy. The plan is that I go back to the animals and tell them that I've got rid of the tigers. They won't believe me so I'll say, "Come and look for yourselves," and I'll lead them all to the castle where the tigers will be lying in wait for them.'

The vultures thought about this for a moment. They liked the idea of picking at the bones of one plump pig, but they liked the idea of picking at the bones of *lots* of animals even more.

'Okay,' said the vultures. 'But make sure you bring back plenty of animals.'

'I will,' said Splodge, sighing with relief. And then his heart started to race again, for one of the vultures said, 'But, to be on the safe side, we'll fly above you to make sure you don't try to double-cross us.'

'Very well,' said Splodge sadly. And then he realized he hadn't a clue which way to go. 'Oh dear,' he said, 'I think I'm lost.'

Then a squeaky voice above him said, 'Excuse me, can I be of assistance?'

Splodge and the vultures looked up. In the darkness they could just see an ugly face hanging upside-down. 'I'm Mrs Fruit Bat, and even though I'm as blind as a . . . bat, if you'll excuse the joke, I'm excellent at finding my way round the jungle at night with my special radar system. I'll lead the way back to the animals, if you like.'

'Splendid,' said the vultures. 'We'll follow you, Fruit Bat,' and they flew into the air and waited for her to lead the way.

But Mrs Fruit Bat, instead of flying up into the air, gave a low whistle. There was a flutter and another fruit bat appeared out of the darkness.

'Splodge, meet my husband, Mr Fruit Bat. Now listen,' she said to her husband. 'Would you mind helping us out of a jam by leading the vultures right round the jungle and ending up back at the castle again?'

'Not at all,' said Mr Fruit Bat and he flew up to where the vultures circled overhead. 'Follow me,' he said, and the vultures, assuming that this was Mrs Fruit Bat and that Splodge Pig was running along below, began to follow him.

Meanwhile, Splodge and Mrs Fruit Bat lay low in the undergrowth.

'It's most kind of you to help out, Mrs Fruit Bat,' whispered Splodge. 'Of course I wasn't really going to lead the animals back to the tigers.'

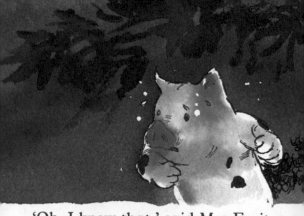

'Oh, I knew that,' said Mrs Fruit
Bat. 'I've heard nothing but good
about you, Splodge, which is why
I'm happy to help.'

After a while, when the vultures
were well on their way, Mrs Fruit
Bat said, 'Right, let's go.' She flew
ahead with Splodge running along
behind, puffing and panting to keep
up.

After an hour or two, the vultures found themselves back at the castle, but Mr Fruit Bat was nowhere to be seen. They realized they'd been double-crossed and squawked with rage.

'That pig will live to regret this,' said the first vulture.

'Yes, but we can't tell the tigers what happened,' said the second. 'They'll be furious with us for making fools of ourselves.'

'Then we'll just have to suffer in silence,' said the third. So they sat and sulked for the rest of the night.

Meanwhile, Mrs Fruit Bat had led Splodge safely back to his friends. At first the animals thought they were dreaming and, when they realized it really was Splodge Pig, they cried for joy. They had never expected to see him again, for no animal had ever before come out of Tiger Castle alive. What an amazing pig!

'Listen everyone,' said Splodge when he'd got his breath back. 'I have finally thought of the best way to rid the jungle of tigers. Now listen very closely. . .'

When the tigers awoke the next morning, they could tell straight away that something was wrong. The jungle was so *quiet*, with no birds singing, no undergrowth rustling.

'What on earth's going on?' they growled, and got up and went outside to have a look.

Suddenly they began to quiver. For the parrot was flying through the jungle screaming, 'Hunters! Hunters!' And then they heard the voice of a *man* saying, 'Well, we've shot a lion and a hippopotamus. What we want to do now is shoot lots of tigers. I could just do with a tiger-skin rug in my sitting room, especially one that belonged to one of *these* tigers.'

And then they could hear gunfire. BANG! went the gun. And then BANG! BANG! And suddenly all the animals were charging out of the jungle to escape the hunters, a look of terror (although it was only pretend) on their faces.

The tigers didn't wait to see more. They all turned, except for King Snarlalot, and ran and ran until they reached the sea, and they swam and swam until they reached an island. The vultures went too. The island was covered with green slimy snakes.

You will have to use your imagination as to how they got on with these snakes, for neither the tigers nor the vultures were ever seen or heard of again.

So Splodge's trick had worked. For a trick it was, as you've probably guessed. Splodge had taught the parrot to imitate the farmer's voice, and the gun fire was nothing more than the bangers he'd picked up in the farmyard.

What a commotion there was as the animals were reunited with their plump babies. Splodge watched, smiling. What a happy pig he felt, for he had managed to rid the jungle of the tigers. His dream had finally come true.

King Splodge

All the animals were shouting,
'SPLODGE PIG FOR KING!
SPLODGE PIG FOR KING!'
Gorilla called for silence and said,
'Splodge, we are all agreed that, if
you would like to be, you should be
our new king.'

'It would be a great honour,' said Splodge and he turned to King Snarlalot. 'That is, as long as you don't mind.'

King Snarlalot said he would be only too delighted to stop being king, and handed his crown over to Splodge.

'I would like to appoint you Royal Gardener,' said Splodge.

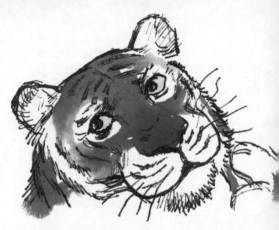

King Snarlalot's smile broadened. 'I want everyone to forget I'm called King Snarlalot,' he said. 'From now on I want to be called Tulip. And may I make another suggestion? The castle should be repainted white with black splodges!'

All the animals laughed and cheered.

182

Meanwhile, back in the Great Hot White Desert, Camel was worried about Splodge Pig. Ever since he'd watched him disappear off towards the jungle, he had been wondering how his friend was getting on. In the end, curiousity got the better of him. He had to find out for himself if Splodge was all right. So he set off into the jungle.

Now Camel was the wrong shape for walking through jungles, and his hump kept getting caught up in vines and branches. But what was really worrying him was that he hadn't yet met any animals. He walked and walked until suddenly he heard loud cheering. He walked towards the cheering and then his mouth dropped open in amazement. For there was Splodge, with a crown on his head, addressing all the animals.

'From now on,' Splodge was saying, 'this will be a peace-loving, happy jungle,' and everyone shouted, 'Hurray!'

When King Splodge caught sight of his friend Camel, he ran over to him and, in a rather unking-like manner, kissed him on his nose. 'My dear, dear friend,' he said. 'You see, I told you that one day I'd be King of the Jungle. You must stay for as long as you like.' Then he said to the other animals, 'It was all thanks to Camel that I came to the jungle in the first place. So I'm sure you will all make him feel very welcome.' Then everyone cheered again.

Now an ordinary story about an ordinary pig would end like this: 'Splodge woke up, rubbing his eyes. He was back, safe and sound, in his pigsty at Lemon Tree Farm. What a lovely dream he'd just had, about being King of the Jungle. . .'

But this is no ordinary story, and Splodge is no ordinary pig. For it all really did happen, and an excellent King of the Jungle he made too. The animals were all very proud of him, and told their babies, who told their babies, and their babies were told about him too. What better animal could they have had as king, than one who could make a sad crocodile laugh, walk across the river without sinking, make a water melon explode with a bang, and send coloured stars up into the sky? But best of all, he was the one who had thought of the way to rid the jungle of tigers.

Now and again, as Splodge sat on his throne discussing important matters with Queen Warthog, and his chief advisers Gorilla, Hippo, Camel, and Mr and Mrs Fruit Bat, he thought back to Lemon Tree Farm and the pigs who all told him he was useless. And he thought to himself, 'If only they could see me now.'

189